Words to Know Before You Read

bark

giraffe

ha ha

honk

hyenas

lion

mew

panda

penguins

roar

www.rourkepublishing.com

Edited by Luana Mitten
Illustrated by Robin Koontz
Art Direction and Page Layout by Renee Brady

Library of Congress Cataloging-in-Publication Data

Koontz, Robin
 Old McDoggle Had a Zoo / Robin Koontz.
    p. cm. -- (Little Birdie Books)
 Includes bibliographical references and index.
 ISBN 978-1-61741-813-6 (hard cover) (alk. paper)
 ISBN 978-1-61236-017-1 (soft cover)
Library of Congress Control Number: 2011924664

Rourke Publishing
Printed in the United States of America, North Mankato, Minnesota
060711
060711CL

www.rourkepublishing.com - rourke@rourkepublishing.com
Post Office Box 643328 Vero Beach, Florida 32964

Old McDoggle
Had a Zoo

Written and Illustrated by
Robin Koontz

Old McDoggle had a zoo
E-I-E-I-O.
And in this zoo,
he had a panda
E-I-E-I-O.

With a bark bark here
and a bark bark there
here a bark, there a bark
everywhere a bark bark.

Old McDoggle had a zoo
E-I-E-I-O.

And in this zoo, he had some hyenas
E-I-E-I-O.

7

With a ha ha here
and a ha ha there
here a ha, there a ha
everywhere a ha ha.

Old McDoggle had a zoo
E-I-E-I-O.
And in this zoo, he had a giraffe
E-I-E-I-O.

9

With a mew mew here
and a mew mew there
here a mew, there a mew
everywhere a mew mew.

10

Old McDoggle had a zoo
E-I-E-I-O.

And in this zoo, he had some penguins
E-I-E-I-O.

With a honk honk here
and a honk honk there

here a honk,
there a honk
everywhere a honk honk.

Old McDoggle had a zoo
E-I-E-I-O.

15

And in this zoo,
he had a lion
E-I-E-I-O.

With a roarrrrrrrrr here
and a roarrrrrrrrr there
here a roar, there a roar
everywhere a roarrrrrrrrr.

Old McDoggle had a zoo
E-I-E-I-O.
And in this zoo, he had a bed
E-I-E-I-O.

18

With a good night here
and a good night there
here a good, there a night
everywhere a good night.

Old McDoggle had a zoo.
Good night!

After Reading Activities

You and the Story...

What animals are in McDoggle's Zoo?

Are Old McDoggle's animals real animals or stuffed toys?

Write a story about your favorite zoo animal or stuffed animal.

Share your zoo story with a friend.

Words You Know Now...

What animal makes each sound? On a piece of paper, write each sentence and fill in the missing animal name.

"Mew, mew," says the _____.

"Honk, honk," says the _____.

"Roarrrrrrrrr," says the _____.

"Ha, ha," says the _____.

"Bark, bark," says the _____.

Animal names:
penguin   lion   giraffe   hyenas   panda

You Could...Visit a Zoo or Pet Store

- Decide if you are going to visit the zoo or a pet store.

- Before your visit write a list of what you think you will see.

- After visiting the zoo or pet store write a new version of Old McDoggle using the names of the animals you saw and the sounds they made.

- What was your favorite part?

- Tell a friend about your favorite part of your visit to the zoo or pet store.

Old McDoggle had a pet store

E-I-E-I-O.

And in this pet store, he had a _____

E-I-E-I-O.

With a _____ _____ here...

About the Author and Illustrator

Robin Koontz loves to write and illustrate stories that make kids laugh. Robin lives with her husband and various critters in the Coast Range mountains of western Oregon. She shares her office space with Jeep the dog, who gives her most of her ideas.

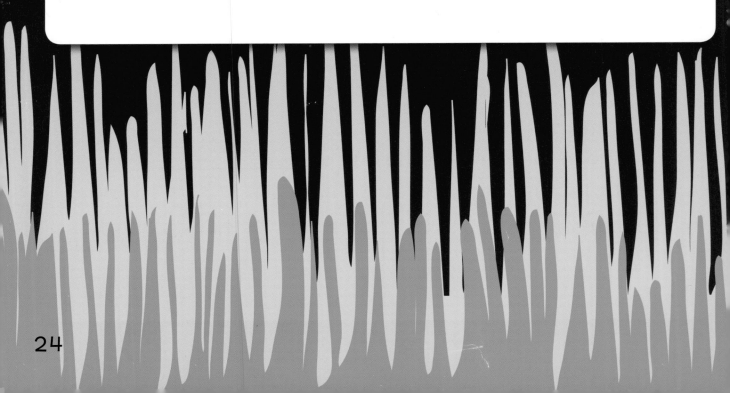